D1621501

Dozi the Alligator Finds a Family

by Daniel Boris

Illustrated by Nicola Sammarco

Dozi the Alligator™

For Rachel and Jake.

HERITAGE BUILDERS PUBLISHING

©2015 by Daniel Boris
Artwork by Nicola Sammarco

First Edition

Published by:
Heritage Builders Publishing
Clovis, Monterey California 93619
www.HeritageBuilders.com
1-888-898-9563

ISBN: 978-1-941437-56-8

Printed and bound in the U.S.A.

Dozi the Alligator ™

In southern USA
in a marshland real cozy,

far from where people stay
lived a gator named Dozi.

On most hot summer days
in the swampy green grasses,

he would wallow and play
as days passed like molasses.

But Dozi's favorite part
of the day was the night,

for that was the time
to see loud, colored light!

Bright-bursting blossoming flowers began popping!

In the sky it all started with no sign of stopping!

He'd hear "Ooo!" He'd hear "Ahh!"
Distant voices would shout.

So Dozi went off to see
what the fuss was about.

The gator was sneaky
like little gators can be,

and Dozi found a way in
so nobody would see.

Dozi hid himself well
beneath big, branchy trees,

under colorful flowers
and some nicely trimmed leaves.

And it wasn't much longer until the place came alive.

So many strange things to see when the people arrived!

Dozi was so amazed!
How could all of this be?

These people were all laughing;
so much smiling and glee!

Some even wore animals
on their clothes, he could see!

So Dozi decided
how bad could they be?

And right at that moment
with a gleam in his eye

Dozi gator decided
to give this new world a try.

In a flash he jumped in
underneath the strange buggy,

where a young person rode
not too far from his mommy.

And Dozi hid in that place
all day until dark,

'til they returned to their car
just outside of the park.

Then he timed it just right;
he moved fast! He was cookin'!

Dozi snuck into the car
when nobody was lookin'.

The family packed up their stuff
with no way of knowing

that "Dozi" was the name
of the thing they were stowing.

With vacation now over
and kids no longer giddy,

parents began the long drive
back home to the city.

Then Dozi popped up and said,
"Hey, Kid! I'm talking to you!

Move over and make
some room for me, too!"

Byron Hoxwinder exclaimed,
"Wow! A gator! Is this true?"

Dozi chuckled and said,
"What was your first clue?"

All the others were busy
concentrating on things,

like driving and reading
and electronic blings.

So it's really no wonder
that right there in the back,

sat Dozi and Byron
just enjoying a snack.

Dozi now wore a red shirt.
Why that was is not clear.

Did he find it in luggage,
that he'd been hiding near?

The two of them talked
passing time on the trip,

chewing cheddar cheese crackers
and handfuls of chips.

As the sun started rising
the journey came to a close.

And Byron laughed at the cheese
on Dozi's fingers and nose.

Then dad shouted out, "Wake up! We're back!

Now let's all lend a hand and begin to unpack."

Byron's eyes opened wide and his face showed fear.

How would his family react to a gator being here?

Dozi said, "Kid, don't worry.
I think this shirt will do.

It's like a disguise
that people can't see through."

Byron wasn't quite sure
if that would be true.

Will Dozi's disguise work?
I don't think so. Do **YOU**?

HERITAGE BUILDERS PUBLISHING

First Edition 2015

Published by Heritage Builders Publishing
Clovis, Monterey California 93619
www.HeritageBuilders.com 1-888-898-9563

ISBN: 978-1-941437-56-8

Printed and bound in the United States of America.

Supports Common Core Standards:
Writing: W.2.1,3,5,6
Speaking & Listening: SL.2.1,1a,1b,1c,2,3,4,5,6
Reading Foundations: RF.2.3,3b,3c,3e,4,4a,4b,4c
Language: L.2.2,2d,3,3a,4,4a,5,5a,5b,6
Reading Literature: RL.2.1,2,3,4,5,6,7,10

Coming **August 11, 2015!**

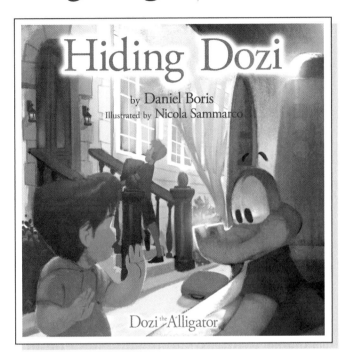

Hiding Dozi by Daniel Boris

In this second book in the *Dozi the Alligator* series, the Hoxwinder family arrives home after a long overnight drive from their Florida family vacation. Dozi remains undetected as the rest of the family is busy unpacking the minivan. Young Byron–panicking about what might happen if his parents discover Dozi–decides to continue hiding the little gator.

The fun continues!
August, 2015